TALES OF RESISTANCE

A YEAR OF STORIES

BY HIROMI COTA

BLUE FORGE PRESS
Port Orchard, Washington

Tales of Resistance: A Year of Stories
Copyright 2019, 2021
by Hiromi Cota

First eBook Edition March 2021
First Print Edition March 2021

Cover design by Brianne DiMarco

ISBN 978-1-59092-956-8

For information about film, reprint or other subsidiary rights, contact blueforgegroup@gmail.com

Blue Forge Press is the print division of the volunteer-run, federal 501 (c)3 nonprofit company, Blue Forge Group, founded in 1989 and dedicated to bringing light to the shadows and voice to the silence. We strive to empower storytellers across all walks of life with our four divisions: Blue Forge Press, Blue Forge Films, Blue Forge Gaming, and Blue Forge Records. Find out more at www.BlueForgeGroup.com

Blue Forge Press
7419 Ebbert Drive Southeast
Port Orchard, Washington 98367
blueforgepress@gmail.com
360-550-2071 ph.txt

*Dedicated to my spouse Randi, for always believing in me,
my parents, for making sure I never went hungry for food or books, and
teachers everywhere.*

TABLE OF CONTENTS

Tales of Resistance

A Year of Stories

by Hiromi Cota

Inside the Blue Circle

The bathroom faucet dripped languidly.

Tip-tap

Tip-tap

A cat loafed on the edge of the sink, her paws tucked underneath her body as she observed each pair of drops. Her eyes gazed into the string of twin worlds created by each faucet drip. Birthing as individuals. Chasing one another as they fell through the air. Fracturing into dozens of new worlds on the basin. Looking up to their descendants as the cycle begins anew. Astra's furry tuxedo bristled and relaxed with each cycle, her tail marking time as morning crept into the tiny apartment.

Tip-tap

Tip-tap

Astra stretched a curious paw towards the faucet's drips, experimenting for the millionth time with what the water would feel like against her fur. A shift of the air injected warnings into her mind and she froze before making contact with the water. Her head flicked to the side and stared at the bed. One of the human lumps she shared the apartment with had begun stirring. The lump stretched and resumed lumping with exasperation.

"Meow?" Astra questioned of the human.

& groaned, rolling out of bed, barely escaping the mattress that felt more like pudding than foam this morning. Their feet entered an uneasy alliance with the floor, chilly faux tile on concrete that extracted heat as its part of the bargain. Each passing moment made the alliance more bearable, but not less regrettable. & pulled their body to the elderly folding table that had long dreamt of being a kitchen.

"Oh, good," & sighed as their bleary eyes found focus on the viewport on the side of the electric kettle. There was still water. & flicked the kettle's switch, the first step of the tea-manifesting ritual. Forcing their eyes to take in the rest of the items on Kitchen, they found the bag of buns. But, before their hand could close on it, the world of sleep took one last shot at &.

A sudden yawn forced their eyes closed and their mouth open to noiselessly roar at the morning for interrupting dreams. They retrieved two buns from the bag and looked back at the bed. A smile birthed on their face as @ scooted closer to the warm spot that had, until recently, held &. They could see @'s face swirl through disappointment to the inevitable and annoying conclusion that it was time to be awake.

Neon Gods, they're cute.

"Tea?" the annoyed @ in the bed inquired.

"Just started the water. Give it a few."

"Bleh. Who the hell invented mornings, anyway?"

"I mean, you know my feelings on time."

"Pfft." @ forced their feet to join the alliance with the floor. Their feet stretched and flexed before striding to the plastic shelving beside Kitchen. Dancing their fingers along the drawers, @ found and retrieved the perfect bergamot tea for banishing the morning brain fog. "Are those European buns still good?"

"I hope so. I don't think European-style buns needed to be refrigerated." & gave them a quick sniff and squeezed them. Generally, wheaty, yeasty, and sweet with a soft, dry texture. "Yeah, they seem fine. These might actually be American."

"What's the difference?" @ scooped up a pair of mugs and trudged to the bathroom to rinse them under the faucet. The sudden change in water pressure earned a dirty look from Astra, who hopped off the sink and sauntered past @, slowing to flick the human's ankle with her tail on her way out. The cat flounced to the bowls, arriving just in time to sit and look annoyed, despite & already having Astra's food bag in hand before the cat even left the bathroom.

"I don't know," conceded &. "Maybe it's like the difference between Japanese gyoza and Korean mandu?"

"Tofu?"

"No, I mean- never mind." & arrived at Astra's bowls, topping both the food and water off, though they knew the water would go untouched so long as the faucet's show continued. "You're such a weird cat," chuckled &. They scratched Astra behind her ears, and then began excavating the pile of clean laundry. & struggled into their binder, squeezing their body into something like the right shape. After a few moments, a gray hoodie, and a pair of ill-fitting blue jeans, Alex&er stood frowning near the pile, his fingers twisting through the air, seeking seams in the fabric of Reality. Golden sparks rained down from where & bruised Reality.

"Alex&er? What are you doing?" asked @, buying time to back up to their dresser, perfectly knowing they weren't going to like what their partner had to say.

"Oh, I'm gonna break it, babe."

"Break what?" they asked, already dreading the answer. They jerked open the dresser and dragged clothes onto theirself.

"I'm gonna break time."

"Again?"

Alex&er nodded and grinned.

"All right, but I'm not putting on a gender this time," @ sighed as they shoved their body into a soft black long-sleeved top.

"You don't have to. You never have to do that for me," winked Alex&er.

"Ugh. Fine." M@ threw a scarf around his neck and crammed his feet into boots.

"I meant it when I said you didn't have to," Alex&er said during a brief window of seriousness.

"Yeah. I know. That just makes it-," @ cut theirself off. "Never mind." N@alie tugged a beanie onto her head. "Today's not a scarf day."

"Not a boy day, you mean?"

"Shut up. Let's go break time or whatever."

Alex&er and N@alie started cleared off the ritual space. Astra supervised. They shoved their various belongings out of the way and fought back the accretion of random junk. Books to the left. Cords to the right. Things that looked edible under Kitchen. Whatever the hell that thing with the knobs was into the trash. After a few minutes of something resembling cleaning, they had freed the vaguely defined circular region of the apartment dedicated to magic. The untiled concrete area bore signs of years of weirdness. Smeared remnants of chalk circles splaying out in overlapping arrays. Salt stains. And an outer circle of blue paint surrounding it all.

The lovers stepped over the blue line.

N@alie knelt. Her part in the spell was security. It was her job to keep Alex&er safe while he screwed with the rules of this dimension. Her hands folded against each other, as she centered herself. Alex&er began crawling around N@alie, orbiting between her and the edge of the blue circle. His fingers traced the inner edge as he moved. Visual echoes of his fingertips started drifting behind them. Soon, an uncountable number of translucent Alex&er fingers followed the presumably real ones attached to his hands.

He swung his hands apart, outlining a circle's arc, and the world outside the blue circle drained of color. Kitchen looked muted. Grayish. Reality itself began to surrender its hold on the apartment, while Alex&er and N@alie became crisper, better defined and more vibrant. The concrete beneath them dropped away, revealing the Milky Way. Yet, they did not fall. Their place in the universe had already been found. Instead, the circle expanded and swallowed the entire Earth.

Alex&er stood in the vacuum of space, his hands glowing with nameless colors, tones that reality had forgotten millions of years ago. N@alie twirled as she rose to her feet, swirling in a full circle, watching the ancient colors surge upwards with her. The pair turned around each other, twin planets orbiting the center, while the universe outside the circle faded to pencil sketches.

&@ opened their eyes. Or at least something that worked like eyes. Their vision flooded with the blackness of space, the nuclear energy of stars, and the dreams of trees. A celestial tapestry wove itself in every direction. Towards @&. Upwards. To the left. Flirwards. To the zir. Even as they gazed upon Reality shaping itself, writing and rewriting itself, they saw theirself embedded within it, the universe stretching towards an understanding of itself. A sphere of life and energy with neither an inside nor an outside. A Klein bottle of energy, matter, and things unknown. The fabric of the universe fluttered as if in response to something beyond &@'s perception.

Motes reclined and tumbled past @&. Lavender ones glittered with secrets untold. White ones danced to an unknown beat. Green motes sailed in random arcs, like lightning swinging from pendulums.

Are those stars? Dust? Souls?

Who knows?

Neither of us apparently. Neither of me?

&@ would have shrugged it they'd had a body.

How long will it take this time?

For Time to repair itself? No idea. I don't even know how much time is passing now.

If those things are stars, we've been here longer than the Earth has existed.

Is that scary?

No. Because I'm not alone. We're not alone? How many of us are there?

Does it matter?

It does. To me, at least.

I was two when we dropped through the seams. I think it's just me in there. Us, I mean.

The Universe roared, stabbing Reality through with tremors. The motes exploded in fragments. And the fragments unified.

Everything fell.

Tip-tap
Tip-tap
"Mew?"

Alex&er and N@alie woke gasping on the floor, their bodies limed in sweat, smoke, and magic. Not for the first time, N@alie wondered if what she'd experienced were real. She rolled her eyes at herself. *Does it really matter? I experienced it. Hell, we both did. If that's not real, what is?*

N@alie pushed the floor away, arriving at a sitting position, looking at her still supine partner.

"Why do you keep wanting the break time?"

Alex&er flopped onto his side, looking up at N@alie. His eyes held swirling galaxies as he fumbled for an answer. He ejected his hoodie and dug his fingers into his binder to peel it off, suddenly uncomfortable with it.

"Because … in that formless moment, that void between the ticks of the clock, I know who I am. Like, I know it doesn't make sense to yearn for an experience where I don't have a body, but—Just for that frozen moment, there's nothing that *isn't* me. Before reality comes rushing back, I don't feel like an & that has to choose—or realize—if today is a boy day or a girl day or neither. I'm just me."

"But, you're not just you there; I'm there with you. I'm *you*, too," N@alie raised an eyebrow as she pulled off her beanie, letting it fall to the floor.

"You know what I mean, though, right? Like, there's no us and no them; it's all the same thing. Everything belongs. Everything's *right*, you know?"

"Yeah, I feel like that when we kiss." @ pulled their lover into their arms and kissed them.

And time stood still again.

Transmission

"Ugh."

Ess wobbled through the night, their barely conscious brain doing its best to keep them upright on the path to the bathroom. The light snapped on.

"Ow. Fuck, that's bright. What the fuck. Why even. Oh." Ess paused, their eyes settling on the mirror, finally feeling the Spectator. "One of you. So, that's why I'm awake. To provide you with an insight into how the other 90% live? Well, you're in for a fucking treat. You'll get to tell all your friends about how you Specced a real-life Deviant," they jeered, arms out of their sides, thrusting their breasts threateningly at the mirror before flicking their hips forward. Ess wasn't sure if their Spectator could feel their penis' bounce, but the Spec probably saw it.

A dozen miles away, sensory processors aggregated the data transmitted by Ess' implants, neural impulses translating into sights, sounds, and feelings, before making their way Uptown. Somewhere, a wealthy Spectator experienced the world through Ess' eyes. Maybe even feeling the world through their skin, if the Spectator had the right upgrades to their body and their Entertainment Feed.

Using the mirror, Ess made creepily defiant eye contact with their Spectator as they took their morning shit and wiped. It wasn't until they washed their hands that the first message crawled into the corner of their vision.

What's your name?

"The fuck does that matter? You're paying to use my body, not to be my friend."

Why so mad?

"I have to rent my body to you people because it's the only work left. It's transmit or starve for people like me. Should I smile and put on a pretty face? Work my way up to being a house slave?"

But, slavery's illegal.

"Is it?"

The text crawl paused, giving Ess time to slip on a black knee-length skirt, pulling on a matching sweater over their chest.

Don't you ever want to be one or the other?

"If you want me to put out that kind of emotional labor, we're going premium for this session." Ess' hand snapped towards their feed controller, seizing the plastic box.

I'll pay it.

"Correct." Ess punched up the price. The shadow in their head dropped off for a moment. Ess breathed out a profane sigh. "Fuuuuck." Their feet padded towards the living corner.

Ess felt someone watching over their shoulder again. The Spec had approved the increase in charges.

"If I wanna be a boy, I'm a boy. If I wanna be a girl, I'm a girl."

What are you right now?

"I'm me, asshole. I'm just me."

Non-binary?

"If you want to put a label on it. Sure." Ess dropped into the blob of foam that someone once thought might be able to make it as a couch.

You don't like labels?

"Kid, what part of this session would lead you to think I liked labels, guidelines, rules, or any outside force telling me who or what I am?" Ess wormed their way over the factory-rejected couch into a reclined position, staring at the mirror on the ceiling. Their eyebrow tugged skeptically upwards, as they gave the Spec a full-length view of their clothed body. "You're a baby queer, aren't you?"

Queer's a bad word.

"No, it's not, but I won't point the word at you if it bothers you. You've never seen someone like me before, have you?"

On the EF. Maxi Fran.

"Good ole Maxi." Ess smirked. "Talked to it?"

My parents aren't *that* rich.

Ess laughed, a smile finally coming out.

But, no. I've never talked to someone like you. Someone like us.

"What's it like up there? A baby gets identified as having a brain/body mismatch and a machine spits out a hormone pill?"

Patch. We use patches now.

"Great. And that works for a lot of folks. Obviously, not everyone gets to take the patch, certainly not down here. Some have to transmit to get enough credit for the hormonal therapy. What happens to people like you?"

It's not a mismatch.

"So, no patch." They crossed their arms under their breasts, and hmm-ed thoughtfully.

No patch. Is this what a normal day is for you?

"Talking to someone who doesn't understand me in exchange for food and rent money? Yeah. Pretty much. I usually swear more and wear less, though."

Why?

"Because most rich weirdos who end up on my part of the Transmission Market want a sassy bitch with a dick. Everyone in their lives showers them with fake praise and love. They want something real. Something raw. Something scandalous. Or maybe they're used to everyone folding the second they raise their voices and want someone to fight back. Or any of another dozen or so psychological profiles."

Wait, are you a psychologist?

"You think I'd be doing this if I had a license?"

Well, you could be a grad student doing research.

"There's no Human Subjects Board in the world who'd let me datamine the behavior of the 10%. No, I'm just a skin worker."

But, you could be more!

"Yeah, I've heard that before. Hell, I hear it almost every day. Clients. Spectators. People like you, who see a strangely articulate slut and can't wait to live out a savior fantasy." They threw a dramatic hand to their forehead and swooned deeper into the couch. "Oh, please! Save me from this horrible life of sin!" They cocked an eyebrow at the mirror, sneering at the Spec through their eyes. "Save yourself, kid. I live here."

They—my parents made the choice for me as a baby. They had the doctors cut me into a boy. I'll never look like you. I'll never be the right me.

"Fuck off. You have the credit to be Spectating, you have the credit to have a body clinic do whatever you want. Probably enough to get gills and a mermaid tail or some shit."

Rebreather.

"What?"

Rebreather. The mermaiders use implanted rebreathers, not true gills.

"Fuck off," they said again.

No, you fuck off. Life's hard for people like us everywhere. I'm not going to play Suffering Olympics. You'd win, but that's not the point. Our parents fucked up our lives. I'm just trying to figure out who I am and how I get to be comfortable in my own skin.

"So why are you here on the Market? Why wouldn't you just plug into one of the support channels out there? Billions of people on this world. Every one of them's online at least a little bit. You're trying to tell me that there's not support group or ten out there for us?"

Mom knows what feeds I access. I can't go there. Last time I tried, I got Regulated into sadness for a full hour.

"A full hour of being sad. Wow," Ess deadpanned. "So, you can't look for help from peers, but you can talk to me because no one blinks twice about a—I'm guessing—teen boy Spectating a whore?" Ess flung their arms over their head and shook them into stretch like they were pushing back reality. "Ugh. Fuck this world. And the people in charge of it."

I gotta go. I got class. Ess gave the Spectator a thumbs up and focused their gaze on it until their eyes were no longer being rented.

"Porn before therapy? How the fuck did those assholes end up in charge of the world?"

DEAD SHIFT

You ever go out to eat at a restaurant and stuff yourself? Like, you knew you shouldn't have that extra basket of bread before the meal, but it was free, so you asked for it and finished it while navigating your way through the main course? And then they asked if you wanted dessert. And you didn't. But, they brought out a fucking cart full of delicate cakes and pies anyways. The sweetness flowed over the table, stealing your willpower, and you said yes.

A few clinks of a fork against the plate later and you felt like you could just be rolled out of the place, because your feet sure as hell weren't going to get the job done. They were so far away from you now. Couldn't even see them with your belly in the way. Or, at least that's how it felt.

Then. The check.

And a few starlight fucking mints.

Any other time, some candy mints would have been lovely, but no one asked for you, mints. Didn't even want the damn dessert, but it was too late for that. And, now, mints?

No. No! Fuck off, mints. I'll just shove you in my purse and forget about you.

That's what Sunday morning at the shop feels like. That's what now feels like. The useless bit tacked on at the end of a long week. After the first five days of my work week, I'm already full. I sure as shit don't need another day. For that matter, neither does the shop. So, it's like a mint for me *and* the store.

No one ever comes in, so I'm here by myself. Why staff the shop with one person when zero would do just as well? So, I'm here, red-eyed and alone. The only people who're likely to walk through that door before the end of my shift will be some sketchy dude looking to sell a phone or a laptop. To a boardgame store. Yeah... It'll be the highlight of my day if the boss messages me some internet orders. Woo. Printing out shipping labels and packing boxes. Riveting stuff.

I could sweep the sidewalk. Am I that bored? Maybe? Hell. I don't know. It's not the day to do it according to the work chart, but it could sure use it. Eh. Fuck it. I'll just go restock the fridge. We kept a minifridge by the counter full of a local soda. As the week went on, various gaming groups would inevitably buy some to keep themselves refreshed as they demolished each other with cards, fought their way through a dungeon together, or whatever.

I checked the refrigerator. Out of root beer. Low on cola. Low on some experimental blue drink with a weird-ass name. Fully stocked on grape soda. Sounds about right. I confirmed that there was no one about to walk into the store, then headed for the employee bathroom. We keep pretty much all our random crap in there on a giant wire shelf. Sodas, cleaning supplies, mugs, and dishes. And a crap ton of water for the water cooler. At the bottom, obviously. Those things were heavy as hell.

I glanced at my reflection in the mirror before grabbing the drinks. Wow. Do I really look like that? Fuck. I look like I've been in a fight with a truck. I splashed water in my face and wiped it clean with a paper towel. How do I look so much better now? Am I seeing shit? I closed my eyes and sighed. C'mon, Min. Get your shit together, girl. I breathed out quickly and opened my eyes.

I looked under-caffeinated, but not under-a-truck-inated, so I guess that'll work. I turned around and grabbed two fistfuls of soda bottles, threading some between my fingers like I was a crane. It didn't exactly feel painless, but it felt efficient.

Thup-thup-thup-thupthupthup

I looked up to the sound of someone hauling ass past the store. I'm not much of a runner, but that looked like a hell of a sprint. Like they were running away from the cops or a mugger or something. This fucking neighborhood. I knelt down to fill up the fridge. The cool air puffed out against my face and hands as I started sliding bottles into their temporary homes. Hmm. Still short one root beer. Eh. I pulled a root beer out of the fridge and closed up.

Note to self. Restock *two* root beers. I stepped behind the counter and scanned the bottle, punching in my employee credit account. Yeah, I'm sure that I could just take the bottle and not pay the store, but that's a dick move. Why punish the store just because I'm bored and kind of thirsty?

Ding-ba-ding

"Welcome to Arthur's Games. How can I aid your quest?" my mouth instincted before I even looked up from ringing up my soda.

"I'm here for you," a raspy whisper of a voice replied. I looked up, squinting against the morning sun behind the man. The glare kept me from being able to focus on his face, but he was wearing a long, tan trenchcoat. Weird choice given that it was warm enough outside for me to run the air conditioning in the shop.

"Yeah, we're not that kind of store, Mister. Nice cosplay, though."

He oozed towards me, his feet silently propelling him the ten feet from the door to the counter. His hand spilled across the counter, reaching for mine. I stood back, yanking my palms away from the leather driving gloves of the stranger. They matched his coat, which might have been stylish if his demeanor didn't make me want to stab him with a fork.

"Hey! I don't know what kind of games you're looking for, but I don't think we have them."

"I'm not looking," he breathed, "for games. I'm here for you."

"This is a game store. We sell games," I verbally shoved at him. "Not people." Fucking great. A creeper. At least this one smells better than usua- Oh. Fuck. No. Never mind. His stench of rotten eggs marinaded in toxic gym socks punched me in the nose. "Have you checked out the shelter over on 9th? They have showers and laundry."

"You have to come with me!" He lunged around the counter, driving glove clawing towards me like a greasy beartrap.

I dashed backwards, kicking a stool at him and backed up into the strategy game aisle. Fuck. I didn't grab the store phone and I don't want to reach for my mobile. It might set this guy off even worse. No, I just need to speak firmly and ask him to— Is that a fucking snake in his sleeve?

"You have been chosen," he shouted, his voice protesting against the effort, then he surged towards me, both arms up now, revealing that, yes, that was indeed a fucking snake. He had a snake for his left arm. Or at least a writhing snake for his left hand. Who knows? Not me. I turned and bolted for the staff bathroom, scattering board games into the aisle in my wake.

I slammed the door of the tiny bathroom shut behind me and flicked the handle locked. Not that I expected the frail door to keep me safe. Fuck. Stupid. I should have-

No. No should'ves. Just do.

The handle shook as I went for my phone, no longer worried about setting the man off. I danced my finger over the lock screen, unlocking my phone. The door lurched, a wide gap opening at the top of the frame. Jesus! It doesn't matter who I call; he's going to get in here before they arrive.

I looked around the bathroom. Vacuum cleaner in the corner. Water cooler jammed against the sink. Metal supply shelf full of mugs, sodas, toilet paper, water, spray bottles. Uh, sure. I snatched a bottle of something blue off the shelf, shoved it into the widening gap, and spraying like mad. A howl like a garbage disposal fighting a lion exploded from the other side of the door. Is this guy human? Of course he is. What fuck else would he be?

The howl backed away from the door. Oh, shit. He's going to ram it. The shelf! I jumped up and grabbed the top of the shelf, pulling with everything I had to tip it forwards. Onto the sink. Shit. It might fall onto me if the sink isn't as strong as I thought. It wobbled forwards, but rocked back to its resting space. Shit!

BOOM!

My ears rang with pain as the man turned the tiny bathroom into a drum. Dust flew as the door splintered in a dozen lines, cracked stretching out from the handle in every direction. The door was still there, but a toddler could force it open at this point. I bent down and grabbed one of the giant water bottles for the cooler, straining against the weight as I slid it in front of the door. It wouldn't hold the door, but maybe it'd- I jumped at the shelf again, gripping tight and swinging hard. It stretched towards me, then I felt it start to topple. Yes! Shit! Both!

The shelf started falling towards me in earnest and I had to scramble downwards to avoid getting pinned between the shelf and the sink. Glass exploded overhead and I started getting punched in the head and back. What the fuck?

BOOM!

The thunder of the man's charge exploded the door, the wood around the lock flying into the bathroom. I could hear at least part of the door swing inwards freely, but the rest of it thudded against my shelf, inches from my face. A bottle of grape soda rolled off of my back and in front of me. Well, at least I know what had punched me now. I clutched the bottle, hoping I could use it somehow. With the remnants of the door in my face, I couldn't see much. I sure as hell couldn't see him. Could he see me? I was trapped and on all fours, but maybe he couldn't get me.

His stench began to flow into the room.

"Nonono. You were CHOSEN!" his voice leapt over me and crashed onto the shelf, bowing it towards me. The sink's wooden pedestal moaned at the new strain, threatening to buckle, dropping the shelf and man onto me. His wild eyes strained in their sockets, reaching for me through the black wire cage, spit- venom? dripping from both his lips and his snake arm. His entire body thrashed and spasmed, pounding against the metal, grinding the shelf against the sink's pedestal.

Something glass in the shelf burst and stabbed down into my calf. I swear. If I bleed to death because of grape fucking soda... I couldn't bend far enough to see my calf, but I could see a bead of the filthy liquid from the guy's mouth threatening to drop onto my face.

I lifted my arm to block the spittle. It burned my forearm, and I jerked my arm away, slamming it into the half of the door that covered the shelf's opening. My knuckles winced and I felt something give in my hand. But, the door fell back. I was exposed to the beast. He could just climb off the shelf and get me.

But, with him above me and the door down, there was nothing in between me and the exit. I shoved myself forward, my left arm giving out under the strain, dropping my head against the edge of the toilet.

My vision blurred as I dragged myself to my feet, a flash of white pain lancing through my right calf as soon as I tried to put weight on it. I felt hot breath behind me. His hot breath. That fucking predator. I fell forward, collapsing into the strategy games, my hands clawing at the products to keep me upright. The bathroom shelf crashed and slammed just feet away as I pulled myself away, pawing at the games to stay standing. Two steps left. One step.

KRRSH-KOOM

Don't look. Don't fucking look. That had to be the destruction of the shelf and sink. I didn't need to look. I just needed to get the fuck out. I heard the squeak of a shoe on the bathroom linoleum. He's coming.

I hurled myself from the strategy games to the counter, gripping it tightly, as I hobbled forward, right leg dragging uselessly behind. The door swung open as I swam into it.

The sun was so bright and warm.

I woke to find strangers kneeling over me, snakes crawling over my body, over my mouth. I slapped the one on my mouth away and frantically crawled away backwards.

"Whoa. Easy there."

"Shit!"

The first one turned to the second. "Well, get the mask before someone runs it over." She turned back to me. "Hi. How're you feeling? You know where you are?" The second one vanished around a corner.

It was daylight. I was on the ground outside the shop, the dirt that I'd decided against sweeping coated my palms. There was an ambulance parked in front of the shop, and these two had on uniforms that matched.

"Oh. What the fuck? What happened?"

"Not really sure, uh, Miss?"

"Mx."

"Miss Mix?"

"Uh. No. Not a Miss or a Mister. I'm a Mx." I paused. "Perez."

"Oh, OK, Mx. Perez" She sounded like she got it. "Well, I'm Susan. I'm a Miss. That's my partner over there, Nguyen."

"Got it!" Nguyen dragged himself out from under the ambulance. "Quite a swing you go there. The oxygen mask almost went into traffic."

"Oh, I'm so sorry!"

"No, no. It's OK. Happens all the time."

"It really shouldn't, though," Susan said while side-eyeing her partner.

"Yeah. Yeah. I'll do better next time."

I braced myself against the shop's large display window and looked at my legs. I don't have a giant shard of grape soda sticking out of my leg. They feel sore, but OK. I walked my hands up the wall as I rose to my feet. Susan held a hand near me, in case I needed it, but I managed to stand, and I turned towards the shop and saw... nothing. At least, nothing unusual. My stool was standing by the counter. The bathroom door was intact. There was no snake-handed man trying to kill me. Just ... games. And shelves.

"Well, looks like we're about all wrapped up here. Hey, sweet ink, Miss."

"Mx. They're- They?" Susan asked and I nodded. "They're a Mx. Mx. Perez."

"Thanks," I said to Susan. "Wait. What ink?"

"On your left anterior forearm."

"Save the anterior and posterior junk for the report, Nguyen."

They kept arguing, but their voices faded away as I pulled up my sleeve. There, wrapped around my left forearm was a tattoo of the man's snake arm. It twisted slowly, almost imperceivably, giving my arm a slight squeeze.

I screamed.

THEORY & PRAXIS

Fuck! *BraAaad! I told you not to touch it!*

How the fuck was I supposed to know something was going to happen?

The book was glowing, you asshole. That's a pretty good sign that it has an alarm.

Oh, excuse me, Mister Heistmaster.

Uh! That was a joke! We weren't trying to steal the book! It was just a pretty manuscript, and my friend wanted to touch it. It was a mistake and we're sorry.

You're seriously confessing at the scene of the crime?

It's not a fucking crime! We didn't do anything wrong. Hey! Security? Can you just turn the lights back on? Not being able to see is starting to creep me out.

Like they care. Hell, that might just make them leave the lights out longer.

Whatever. Look. … I just want to get out of here. I have a date.

WhaaAT? Bullshit. Who with?

Victor.

Fucking football team Victor? That dick?

Shut up. He's nice.

Well, I hope he's got a tight END for you.

He's an offensive lineman, ass.

What the fuck are you two going on about?

HOLY FUCKSHIT! **WHO THE FUCK'RE YOU?**

We were alone a second ago!

Yeah, no. I've been here for at least a fucking day. You two (I'm guessing kids) just showed up a minute ago.

You've been SPYING on us for a minute? Who the fuck're you?

Look—fuck. I hate that word now. Listen—

No, you listen, you fucking creeper! What the fuck is going on? Why aren't the lights on?

LISTEN! We're not in the museum anymore.

Are you high? *What the hell are you smoking?*

Take a step, smartasses.

What? **Oh shit.**

Just do it, kid. **Oh shit. Ohshit. Oshit. Oshitoshitoshit**

Brad! It's OK! Brad! Bradbradbrad! Calm down. Just—

Take a fucking step, kid!

What is with you and—

oh...

Ooohhhh.

Where the hell are we?

No idea. But, obviously gravity doesn't fucking work. Either that or our bodies don't. Hell, for all I know, we're dead and we're a bunch of lost souls.

Nononono. I can't be dead. I can't! I can't.

Your buddy's going to pass the fuck out if he keeps freaking out like that.

That's not a thing!

Brad! You're OK! We're both OK. We're just ... I don't know, in a loading

screen. Maybe we're going to Narnia or something!
That'd suck. Narnia was a warzone. **I need to see my granny.**
Lord of the Rings, then! **I can't. No. I'm OK. I'm OK.**
Also a warzone. **I'mOK.M'OK.**
Shut up! You're not helping! Brad! Hey! I'm right here!
C'mon, Brad. Hey! Hey! You with me? **M'OK.M'OK.M'OK.**
m'ok.m'ok.m'ok.m'ok How long does this usually last?
Until he's done. If you think you're **m'ok.m'ok.**
having a bad time listening to him, **m'ok.m'ok.**
just think how HE feels! **m'ok.m'ok.**
Yeah, OK. Fair enough. **m'ok.**

Brad?

Hi.

Uh.

What's your name?

Ron. What's yours, Heistmaster?

Heh. I'm Martín. You have any idea what the hell happened?

You were in the Smithsonian, right? The new exhibit? It wasn't
supposed to be open yet, but I'm guessing you two were as much
nosey shits as I was and just snuck past that silk rope. If they wanted
to keep people out, they'd try harder, right? The book was in the
middle of the new exhibit room, with weird writing on the walls.
Yeah. Like Sanscrit or some shit.

No.

Just, no, Kid.

Sanscrit looks nothing like that. Holy shit. You don't know anything
about other languages, do you? Dammit. Anyways, weird writing. Like
I've never seen. And it glowed. No. Not just glowed. It pulsed, like a
cop car's lights or
The Enterprise's warp core!

Uh… Yeah, I guess. It was red for me, but I guess "warp core" isn't a bad description, especially since it warped us into whatever limbo we're in now.

It was red for us, too. What if—

Yeesss? You gonna finish that thought?

What if the light was pulsing … like a pulse? Like, it was alive?

Y'know what? A day ago, I'd say that was the stupidest fucking thing I've ever heard of, but after the last 24 hours, I gotta admit that I'm open to new ideas. So, let's say the book was alive. Was the book all that there was? Or was it just one part of something bigger?

Bigger?

Like the book was a hand or a **mouth.**

Ah, shit, Kid. So, we just hopped into the mouth of a book monster? Can't say that I saw this on my top five ways that I'd probably go out.

You have a list of ways you're going to die?

Sure. Who doesn't?

Did you say BOOK MONSTER?

Yeah? Is that so weird?

YES! *Kinda.*

Weirder than being in the Smithsonian one minute and then popping out here? Wherever the fuck here is?

Yeah, OK. Fair enough. So, what are we going to do?

What do you mean?

What? **What do you MEAN, what you do mean?**

Look, do you have a body here? 'Cause I don't. Try to touch your nose. Can you do that? Click your heels together? Clap? Can you DO anything? There's no ME. I'm … I'm not me here. I'm not anything.

You're a voice at least. You have to exist.

I can hear you. *We can hear you. We hear you.*

What good does that do?

What doesn't it do? You know how many poor bastards there are out there who wish someone would hear them? Because they're sick or society's too fucked up to give them a chance? How many people are just yelling into the fucking void trying to get an echo back?

~~Ever have a total stranger go up to you and ask you what time it is? Or start talking about their favorite thing? Trying desperately to connect with another human being?~~

Who *the* FUCK **are** *you?!*Who **the** FUCK are **you**?!*Who the **FUCK** are* you?!

BE FAE! DO CRIMES!

Humans say things like, "Be gay! Do crimes!" Which is just terrible.

I mean, which crimes am I supposed to do? There are so many! I've probably done crimes just by being me, but that doesn't count, I'm sure. And how many crimes ought I do? There has to be a specific number. Does it fulfill the request if I just do two? After all, that makes it crimeS. But what if I do the same crime twice? That probably doesn't count. That's not crimes; that's just one crime multiple times. I find this lack of specificity vexing. But I'll document my crimes anyways. After all, if I don't write it down, then it never happened. At least that's what Da said. He'd know. He's been ignoring lots of things that I did without recording.

So, the crime! I picked graffiti. It was loads of fun.

It wasn't easy, though. First, I needed to get paint. The human male at the hardware store did *not* want to sell me any. First, he told me that I needed an adult to buy them for me; said I was too little to be buying spray paint. I assured him that I was big enough to not fly back when I pushed the button. He didn't look like he believed me. Then, he told me that I didn't need 17 cans. I told him that I did if I wanted to do a good job. AND THEN! He said that he didn't take gold coins. Can you believe it?!

He changed his tune when I told him I had lots of them. I made three piles of gold on the counter and his eyes went ... well- You know how when your uncle's been drinking for 17 days and then sleeps for 17 days and you wake him up? How he makes a face like "Auch. What did Aw do?" and you have to tell him that he thought that he'd found the goddess Aine and wanted to be her husband more than he wanted his left ear. But your uncle wanted to be better than King Aulom, so he visited Aine every day, giving her offerings and poems and asking her out dancing. But she said "nay" every time. Until the last of the 17 days, when she finally agreed, and he got the parson out of bed to wed them that very evening. Long story short, my uncle's now married to the red mare in the stables. Yeah, the shopkeeper at the hardware store made that face. My uncle too.

Anyways, the human at the hardware store saw the three piles of gold and said, "That better not be fairy gold!" and took a taste of a coin.

"Oh! Rumbled! You found me out!" I replied, making finger guns at him like I saw on the telly once.

But he scooped up the coins and waved me off. For a second, I thought it might count as a crime when coins turned back into leaves, but I don't think it does. I told him that he'd rumbled me, and he still took the coins. A deal's a deal.

So, I got the spray paint cans and took them to the local constabulary. I also heard humans say "fuck the police" but I'm too young to be doing any o' that. But, the f-word comes with a lot of meanings, so I'm sure that one of them ought to fit what happened next.

I started building a base layer for my graffiti with a great many of the white paint cans. Well, I say "white", but they had daft names like "off-white," "mountain peaks," "dove feather," and other nonsense. After a few minutes, a gent in blue came over and asked me what the hell I thought I was doing. I told him, but he was still mad and tried to take the can out of my hand.

He grabbed the can and jerked this way and that, but it didn't spoil my aim any. I had to stop spraying a few times when he got between the can and my canvas, though. He grabbed my wrist with both hands and held on, but it didn't do him any good. It was a good long while before he got annoyed and reached for a pair of handcuffs. They looked like they might be iron, which was a bit of a fright for me, so I tried to keep my hands safe from his. But he was a tricky one and eventually got a cuff on. Not iron. Whew. He tried attaching the other cuff to my left wrist, but I certainly wasn't going to help him do that.

After a minute of avoiding the other cuff, his face was red, and he was grunting and growling. He was apparently upset at the noises he was making because he secured the other end of the cuff to his own wrist. He said he did it for crying out loud. I guess that's a crime worthy of cuffing. The silly thing was that now that he was attached to me, I just dragged him around the painting as I worked. I'm not sure if that's a crime, but he wasn't happy about it, so I'm pretty sure that I "fucked the police." Mission accomplished. Well, that mission anyways. I still had crimes to do.

I started on with the blues and blue-greens and greens and grays. Strange that two colors ought to have so many words. My painting was really coming together now. I could almost feel the unicorn's restlessness on the surface of the wall. The flare of her nostrils. Hooves yearning to break through the ground.

The blue boy was weeping, crying out for me to let him go.

That didn't make any sense to me. After all, he was the one with the keys, wasn't he? If he didn't want to be attached to me anymore, he could just unlatch the cuffs. It wasn't that far to the ground. I floated twenty feet lower and gave him a "well?" look. He didn't see it because he was crying. Can't say I didn't try, though. I gave the unicorn a tousled mane with a few hundred quick flicks of the can.

An annoying man gargled through a speaker that someone was under arrest. Whoever that was had five seconds to release their hostage. Four seconds. Three. Two. "Do it now!" he said. He was very serious for someone who forgot how to get to one.

"You forgot one!" I helped.

"Come down to the ground and let the hostage go!" he shouted back. I hadn't seen anyone else flying, so it dawned on me that he might be addressing the blue boy. I yelled over my shoulder.

"Oh, I'm not a hostage. I'm OK. I don't know why he attached himself to me, but it doesn't really bother me. He can stay if he wants to."

"No! You! With the pink hair! Drop the hostage!" Apparently, they thought the blue boy was the hostage, which didn't make any sense. I decided to help them for free.

"You're in error. He put these cuffs on us. No one here is a hostage."

"You're under arrest!" he yelled.

"That can't be right," I replied and dug through my hip pouch for the last color I needed.

The man with the speaker yelled something about a fire, but I didn't smell smoke, so I assumed I was upwind of it. Presumably, Speaker Man had many alarming things to yell about today. I wondered if that was his job.

Lightning flew from the ground and struck my blue friend.

He did not appreciate it. Nor did I, since it gave me a mild zap through the cuffs. It happened again. And again. Speaker man said nothing about this strange lightning, so I assumed he was too busy paying attention to the fire to notice. Blue Boy sobbed.

"Aren't you going to get in trouble for crying out loud so much?"

He replied in a language I wasn't familiar with. Whatever tongue it was involved a lot of sniffing.

"You gave me this cuff, so I'm going to keep it, but you clearly own the other half. How about I just split it in the middle?" His head twitched. I'm pretty sure it was because of the lightning striking again. Still counts, though, so I broke the chain between the cuffs. He dropped to the ground faster than he ought to have and landed like a horse plop. I guess the lightning interfered with his flying ability. "Sorry!" I shouted down at him.

I finally found the right color to finish the unicorn and gave my painting a long, bold stroke. Speaker Man's speaker crackled like he was going to be angrily wrong about something again as the 30-foot-tall unicorn whinnied and tore itself free of the police station wall, raining bricks and dust on those below. The speaker stopped crackling, and screams came from below me. The unicorn leapt off of the wall, exposing several floors of the police station. The people inside started screaming, too. I joined them just in case it was fun.

It turned out that screaming *was* fun. Unfortunately, it involved a lot of closing my eyes and raising my head upwards, so I wasn't paying attention when the unicorn ran me over. That hurt. I'm not certain how many ribs I'm supposed to have, but I don't think I have that number anymore. In hindsight, I should not haven painted iron horseshoes on a unicorn. On the plus side, I had definitely performed a crime.

A crime. Just one. So far.

I danced over towards speaker man, who was huddling against a police car. I squeezed his hand and the device inside it. The speaker crackled and I started to sob and wail into Speaker Man's contraption. Crying out loud. Nailed it.

Been gay.

Done crimes.

What else ya got, World?

QUEER 101

Is this the book I need?
It's *a* book you need.
Ugh. Well, how many other books do I need?
"Need" is a value-loaded word with many concepts constellated around it.
Given what you know about me, my current grades, and the books, do I need more books?
Oh, god, yes.
Could have just led with that.

Ehhh.
Pretty sure he needed to screw with you.

Are you done screwing with me?
Oohh, what do you think?
I think that if I say "yes," you'll tell me that I'm too trusting and that you're morally obligated to fuck with me. And if I say "no," you'll say that you feel hurt that I've become jaded against my own personal liberators.
I'm so proud of you right now.   **Beautiful.**
And, I still don't understand why you keep calling yourselves my liberators.

We're saving you from the heteros.
Pretty sure I'm one of the heteros.

Impossible. My gaydar is a finely tuned instrument.

I'm a guy and I like chicks.

You're a man and you like women. If you liked baby chickens, you'd be on a totally different spectrum and journey. Also, I wouldn't help you.

What if I'm totally straight and what you're picking up is just me being weird.

Well, weirdness can qualify as queerness.

Oh, not that definition.

What's wrong with that definition of queer? Wait. What is that definition?

Under that framework, anything outside of a young, white nuclear family is queer. The hegemony of the state depends on the reinforcement of capitalism, vis a vis the workforce producing future workers and consumers. Difference disrupts the state's control especially difference that impacts consumerism and predictable reproduction.

Ugh. Don't say vis a vis. It makes you sound like an asshole.

He is an asshole.

Yeah, but he doesn't need to advertise it.

At any rate, that model of queer indexes race, ethnicity, age, ability and everything else under queerness.

Like, sure, being gay, black, old, poor, and/or in a wheelchair is queer in a sense, but we already have those categories and Kimberlé Williams Crenshaw demonstrated how the social

problems faced by people who belong to more than one marginalized group are different than those who only belong to one. So, why bother trying to collapse those groups into one set when we already have evidence that differences matter?

Who?   *Kimberlé Williams Crenshaw! Intersectionalism is technically part of Feminism, not Queer Studies, but—*

Just read it. If you can mix in sources from other disciplines your professors will love you.

Because they'll think I'm smart?

Oh, no.   *No one's smart in Queer 101.*

Your professors will just enjoy reading your papers more than everyone else's stuff.

Turns out that seeing the same basic argument written with minor word variation is boring as fuck.

How often does that happen?

All the time.   **Literally all the time.**

Is Queer 101 just indoctrinating us, then?

Oh, you caught us.   **So busted.**

Teaching the Straights that the Homos are real life people who get screwed harder by life is hardly indoctrination. It's just— You wanna do the thing?

Yeah, sure.   What's he writing?

Don't worry about it. Look, you want to be a teacher, right?

You've done some shadowing and tutoring?   Yeah.

What's the best part?

Seeing kids succeed. Like, there's thing moment where their eyes light up and they get it. It's the best thing in the world.

BOOM! I'm 3 for 3!   What?

*I wrote likely answers. You said all of them. "Seeing them succeed,"
"eyes light up," and "when they get it."*

**We had no way of knowing what your experiences with teaching
kids were like. We never saw you tutor anyone and we've never
talked about the little rugrats, yeah?**

Then, how'd you know?

*You wanna see four essays that also
have those three phrases?*   **From this week?**

*Some experiences are just universal. The social awakening that
accompanies learning how to not be a dick to queer people is one of
them.*

So, what if I'm just straight?

We'll accept you no matter what.   **You're hella queer,
though.**

Didn't you just point out that differences matter and not everyone
needs to be under the same umbrella?

Ah ha! He caught us!

                           **Congratulations.
You are now a level 2 queer.**

Dammit!

THE DIM

You ever been in a room where the lights seemed to dim for the length of a blink but no one else seemed to notice? There's no *seem to* about it. You saw what you saw. They saw what they saw. These things are true. So, why would you see something different from everyone else?

It's easy to answer that question, though the precise details...? Well, let's leave that to philosophers, religious figures, and quantum physicists. The simple reason they didn't see it? Because they couldn't; they were in the wrong reality to do so. This doesn't mean that you're in the right reality. I mean, your reality hasn't been paying its light bill. What's up with that? C'mon. Get it together.

The people who didn't see the Dim are your celestial neighbors, hanging out in an adjacent reality. You can talk to them and give 'em a high five, but at the end of the day, you'll never see them again. At least, you won't see that version of them. Infinite adjacent realities are tricky like that. But, just because these people'll vanish from your life by the time the moon sets doesn't mean that you have license to be a dick to them. They're still people.

Besides, if learning that your actions have little consequences turns you into an asshole, what does that say about you? That you're only a nice person so long as there's someone bigger than you? Sounds like a waste of humanity. We didn't become top of the food chain in a million universes by being strong; there are dozens of animals that got us beat there. We're not even the top because we're smart. We're number four there. Good, but not running the world good. No, the only thing we do better than anything else in the worlds is cooperate.

Anyways, you've probably guessed that the dim light was more than just a late payment. Sorry about that. Didn't mean to fib; I just wasn't trying to drop all the knowledge on you at once. I mean, I just told you that everything you know about the nature of reality and existence is wrong. Kinda heady. So, the Dim? It means someone in your reality just died. It happens. There aren't that many people in each reality, so it's a big deal. The Dim is kind of like your reality's way of pouring one out for its homie. Because when things die in one reality, they don't get replaced. Sooner or later, your reality's going to be empty. Maybe it's empty now. Sure, you'll still see people, but no one will know the real you; they'll just know the versions of you from other realities.

Sound lonely? It doesn't have to be. Yes, you'll never be the you that other people know. Yes, everyone who enters your life will be a stranger. So, what? You're still you and you can still help shape your world, as well as other ones. Use that human collaboration. Just remember to not treat anyone like they owe you something because they might not. We're all in this together, even when we're off in our own little worlds.

The Light

It's hard to think of a time before The Light. No, not hard, just — well, why bother? Look, if you're reading this, you're looking for an instruction manual, a history, something to indicate what you should do next. And that means that we've failed.

Bear with me here. The Light was neither a natural nor spontaneous event. Nor was it the result of aliens or religious deities of whatever faith coming to set the world straight. We did it. Humans. Ordinary humans.

On June 21st, 0th Year of the Light, at 1:33pm UDP, the Light began. The entire surface of the Earth was lit by an overwhelming white beam. From polar cap to cap, all eight billion of us were blind to the future. Every telescope on the planet overloaded. The Light lasted exactly 23 seconds, after which 128 of the world's wealthiest and most controversial figures were missing. Even more shocking, several of them had been in televised and public appearances at the time, leaving thousands witness to their disappearances.

The days that followed had conspiracy crackpots, intelligence services, religious leaders, and journalists scrambling for the truth.

Nothing any of them hypothesized was remotely true, but that didn't stop the public from panicking. Huge swaths of Earth's people simply refused to work, assuming that the end of the world was at hand. They chose to spend time with loved ones instead of keeping the wheels of industry turning.

Few nations, corporations, and organized religions survived the political fallout of the Light. Even fewer survived the reappearance of some of the missing 128.

The 128 had been stripped of all of their belongings, infected with the common cold, and left to fend for themselves in slums across the world. Most of them were completely incapable of adapting to lives without privilege. Some lashed out at their new neighbors out of fear, xenophobia, or inability to cooperate. Virtually all of these members stopped appearing in the Light Project's surveillance recordings by the end of July. The handful who attempted to ingratiate themselves to the locals fared better, though not without a few deadly cases of pneumonia. All in all, we believe that 102 members of the 128 died from their conditions.

The survivors found themselves 'coincidentally' captured on video shot by travelers, documentary crews, and international aid workers. Rumors that the 128 survived the Light raced nearly as fast the skeptics denouncing the footage as hoaxes. By the time that any of the 128 had serious attempts to document them, the gravity of what had happened hit everyone.

Aliens, God, Gods, *Something* had taken these people from their gilded nests and thrown them into the gutters. Why should any of them return to power? Why should their wealth be restored to them? The Light had stripped them of everything and could do so again at any moment. The next 128 most wealthy, powerful, and cruel fled or were thrown down by their people.

The vast majority of the powerbrokers of the world were

hiding, imprisoned, or dead.

Instead, a new message rose from the people: "Try Harder. Be Better. Help."

"Or something will destroy you," was implied, but rarely stated.

A decade later, the next generation has come of age. They grew up under the Old Ways and saw the Light as children. They knew of little else aside from looking for what they could do to help others, imagining the world not as a dog-eat-dog struggle, but as a world-wide network of beings who could thrive if we all just tried harder, were better, and helped.

I'm closing this log out. There's no more purpose for it. Either the Earth has been fixed, at which point no one will ever read this, or we only bought humanity a few years of global peace, the first years we've ever had in recorded history.

If you're reading this, understand what has happened: The world wasn't turned around by gods or aliens or anything supernatural. Humans made it happen. Not the Light Project. Not me. Ordinary humans who heard the message and took it to heart. People like you.

Even if you don't believe what the Light was and you don't believe me, you can believe that. Humans healed themselves. Everyday people grow the food, pave the roads, and tend the sick. All it took was ignoring the demands of those with plenty and looking after those in need.

Try Harder.

Be Better.

Help.

The Incident at Mason Ridge Valley

No shit, there I was: knee-deep in bullet casings and hand grenade pins. Haw! Naw, I'm just funnin' you. It was ankle-deep, at best.

Anyways, I had a bit of a situation out at Mason Ridge Valley, which is the dumbest damn name for a valley. Listen, you know what a ridge is, right? High part of the ground? Usually in a line? So, there are two sides that go down from there. But, with a valley, two parts go up. There's usually a ridge on each side of a valley is what I'm sayin'. So, why would you name a valley after something that's off on the side of it instead of the river or stream that's probably in the middle? I'd have called it Whisker Stream Valley, but no one asked me. Anyways, Mason Ridge Valley.

Back then, it wasn't part of the city; it was unincorporated, although I'm not rightly sure why corporations got a say in the matter. Eh? Ehhh? Fine. Your mama hated my puns, too. It was unincorporated territory, so it wasn't strictly speaking my job as deputy to go out and do anything out there. Out of my jurisdiction, you see. That didn't mean that I didn't go out there and see what I could do to help. Most of the people out that way weren't bad folks; they just didn't want to be part of the city or were just on their way somewhere else.

These days, the canyon's a techy commercial park, but back then it was basically a hobo camp, or a "homeless encampment", I guess you'd say these days. Travelers from all over, you know? Canyons aren't great to live in during the rainy months, but foraging's easy, especially back then. They were mostly Romani, what ignorant folks call "Gypsies," 'cept that word means Egyptian, which doesn't have nothin' to do with the Roma. Historically, the word "gypsy" got used to talk a whole mess of shit about the Romani, gettin' them into trouble with some evil folks, who didn't take kindly to—the hell was I saying?

Oh, yeah. So, the folks over in the camp were a mix of folks, like they usually are. Mostly Roma, but also some folks actin' like good ole boys from back East, 'cept their accents weren't quite right and they sure didn't look like they were equipped for farmsteadin'. I figured they must've been run outta town somewhere and were lookin' for a fresh start. Can't fault 'em for that, whatever their crimes in the past were.

Officially, the whole damn camp was trespassing on Old Man Ford's land, but we couldn't legally roust them and I didn't give a shit about stoppin' 'em, so Ford just had to accept the fact that there were fifty to a hundred folks livin' off his land at any given time. But, honestly, who cares? Old Man Ford had a couple hundred acres. He could ride for days without seein' anyone aside from his ranch hands, so it's not like he didn't have plenty of other land.

'Course, that didn't stop him from wanting more. He'd paid a whole dollar and twenty five cents for that parcel of land, so he was willing to hire a few gunmen to scare people off their technically unlawful homes. Worse, he didn't care if those guns killed people. For a whole dollar twenty-five cents worth o' land. I'm not joshin' you. That's how cheap land was and how awful rich folks is. He didn't even have any plans for it; he just didn't want anyone else on the land.

How'd I know about the gunmen? Well, 'cause Ford asked me if I wanted in. He asked Sheriff Ke-etch, too, but Bill just laughed in Ford's face. I reckon that made Ford mad as hell, but it's not like he didn't have it coming. An old, white, rich man asking an Indian, excuse me, Indigenous man for help in taking land away from some nomads? You can bet I laughed, too.

I didn't know who else he asked, but I figured it'd be someone with more guns than sense. You know the type: proud of things they didn't do, protective of things they don't have, angry at things that don't affect them a whit. After Sheriff Ke-etch and I got done laughin' and lookin' after things around town, we figured we'd ride out to the Valley and make sure that things were OK out there.

What we saw there when we arrived was just—well, shit. I guess I'll just start with how it felt. We were crossin' the Mason Ridge into the valley a smidge after sundown. We figured if anything was going to happen, it'd be around then, so we'd be right there to put a stop to it in case the hired guns wanted to try their hand at a massacre. It was dark as hell. There was a full moon out, but the clouds weren't helpin' matters a whit. The clouds were patchy, but the sky was more clouds than patch. Besides it being darker than it ought to be, it was damn quiet. Usually, I'd hear some fiddlin' or drums or singin' or something before I even set eyes on the camp. Some kinda music to let us know where we were. But, nope. Not so much as a jingly bell. No fires or nothin', neither. Just this wall of quiet darkness.

I was about to ask Bill if we were in the right place when I heard someone holler out, screamin' like the Devil was after them, watchin' them race up the opposite ridge on the other side of the valley and fall ass over teakettle off the other side. Then, it was quiet again. Bill sucked his teeth and unslung his rifle. I did likewise. Well, the rifle bit. I didn't suck my teeth so much as mutter "What the hell" and say a little prayer.

Even though it didn't make the best tactical sense, I let Sheriff Ke-etch go on ahead. He was a better rider and was far better at seein' in the dark than I was. Some ignorant townies had claimed that because he was Indigenous, he had magic powers that gave him the eyes of a cat, but he just plain spent a lot of time outside. Nothin' magic about that; it's just hard work. Those same damn fools would probably say that it was Swedish magic that gave me big arms instead of a life growing up workin' the land. Anyways, it wasn't a great idea for us to go down one by one, in case we needed to shoot. I wouldn't be able to fire over his head safely. But, again, he could see and ride better than I could, so it's what we did.

We started makin' our way down to the valley floor, horses amblin' down the grassy slope, when his rifle snapped up into his shoulder and he said something in his native tongue. I don't rightly know what it means, but I'd worked with him long enough that I knew it meant something like "Stop moving and pay attention." So, that's what I did. I pulled my rifle up to my shoulder, too, just in case. I didn't figure I'd have anything to shoot, certainly not anything I could safely shoot at, but—well, when your boss gets ready to shoot something, it seems like a bad idea to not be ready yourself.

I still couldn't hear nothin'. Not even a bird or a 'squito. Just the sound of my horse Cassie's breathing: heavier than it ought to be given how slow we'd been moving down the ridge. Maybe she was a mite tense. I sure was. Sheriff Ke-etch had only used that phrase a few times before and it never came before anything nice.

A twig or something snapped, and the Sheriff hollered out for someone to, "Hold it right there!" I couldn't exactly see who was there, but I didn't need to see clearly for me to point my rifle in the right direction and make his threat twice as big. Fortunately, it was off to the side; I wouldn't need to worry about accidentally hitting Bill.

"Just take it easy. We can all get home OK tonight," I added, hoping that a less stern voice might hedge our bets. Bill's tough approach gets most folks to surrender, but every now and then, there's some damn fool who gets his hackles up when challenged or someone who's scared as hell and ready to do somethin' stupid. That's where I come in with my reminder that life isn't just right now; it's also tomorrow, so let's not do something rash.

Either a patch of clear sky popped up or my eyes finally started workin' in the night and I could pick out the outline of the man we were pointing our guns at. It was one of the kids from town, undoubtedly out here to earn a few dollars hurtin' folks. He didn't look like that enterprise was goin' so great.

"You gotta help me, Sheriff!" he wailed.

"Where's the rest of you? Where are the folks who live here?" Bill asked, gettin' straight to the point.

"I don't know. I don't know! Those things are out here! They got Cris and R.B., and I don't know who else, but we gotta get out of here before they come back!" the kid ranted.

None o' this made a whole lot of sense to me, but if the old man's gunslingin' kids got roughed up by the campers, I wasn't gonna cry a whole lot. But, there wasn't no sense in lettin' this kid get beat any more; he'd clearly had enough.

"Y'mind if—" I started to ask Bill.

"Yuh," he responded before I'd even finished.

"All right. Come on up here, tenderfoot." I holstered my rifle and gave Cassie a little nudge with my knees to get her over to the kid. I held my hand out to him while she brought us closer. He hustled towards us, barely not tripping over grasses, roots, and other thick vegetation of the valley. His fingers brushed against mine before he barreled away like he was shot out of a cannon. Some kind of animal snarl shot past me in the same direction, and the little patch of clear sky closed back up.

We were in the moonless dark again. With that animal. Based on the voiceless trashing in the brush, the kid wasn't with us no more.

"We go now, " Bill ordered. He didn't need to tell me, but I'm glad we were on the same page. I drew my pistol. Better for things that were close and fast. Not that I wanted to take a shot while it was so damn dark. I heard a bit of steel on leather that told me the Sheriff had come to the same conclusion. Then, I heard somethin' else. A baritone growl, bass notes stepping down like a hangman comin' off the gallows, lookin' for his next customer.

Then, I heard another.

And another.

"Are we —" I asked just to ask. I already knew the answer.

"Yuh." We were surrounded by those things.

"Cougars?"

"Don't know."

"What'd'you mean you don't know? You know everything in Oregon."

"I know everything *natural* in Oregon."

My horse bucked as she kicked out at something behind us. By the time I'd swung my head and gun to see what it was, it had vanished back into the night. Another baritone wave of a growl creaked to life right behind me as soon as I was facing to the rear. It had to have been right between Sheriff Ke-etch and myself. And then it was somewhere else before my eyes could even point in the right direction. I was going to die out here. My horse knew it, too. Whether it was pure luck or love that she hadn't thrown me off and ran for her life, I'd never know, but Cassie stayed put.

Every time I'd been out here had been a pleasant trip until now. The campers were always kind and polite, sharin' food if they had it, songs if they hadn't. I'd do the same back to 'em. The campers might not have technically belonged here, but they'd made their home along the Whisper. Now, they were probably dead, either from the kids or from whatever these animals were. As terrible as my own imminent death was, I couldn't help but think back to the times I'd checked in on the folks out this way. The music, the meals, the feeling that you could be from anywhere, but if you were in the Valley, you were home.

"Whatever you're whistling, keep it up." I blinked at Bill, realizing that I *was* whistling. One of the songs I used to whistle when the campers asked me if I had something to share. While I whistled, the gallows creak growls were silent. You might be thinking as I do these days, "were those animals actually the campers?" Damned if I know. I'm certainly not one for putting out any rumors of the supernatural that might get someone lynched. I didn't remember the Romani having any stories like this, but they weren't the only campers. I'm not sayin' the allegedly 'good ole boys from back East' were responsible for this mess, but I'm not *not* sayin' it, you understand me? Whatever those things were, they knew me from my song and it made them want to eat me less. I whistled it as long as I could as Bill and I made our way out of there. When my lips gave out, I sang it. I didn't know the words, but I knew the tune well enough. I sang it until my throat cracked and I couldn't no more. By then, Sheriff Ke-etch knew how it went and he took over. The rest of the way home. At least an hour of singin' for each of us.

I don't know when the animals left us, but when we were lit by the yellow gas lights of town, we were alone. The song? Well, I don't know the name back then, just the tune, taught to me by my Swedish

Mormor. I'm sure she tried to teach me the words, too, but I've never have much of a head for languages. Yeah, yeah. The song's name. I'm gettin' to that.

Varulven.

The Werewolves.

I don't think those things were cougars. At least, not full-time cougars.

Mad Tea Party

Author's note: *Public domain works are free to do whatever we want with them. We can get the text, print it out, sew the pages together, and sell the resulting book. We can even make a copy of a famous piece of art, put our personal spin on it, and try to get the new version in a museum.*

Public domain works of art belong to the people. This doesn't mean that we can walk into the Louvre and take the Mona Lisa off the wall; specific copies still belong to specific people. But it does mean that we can make our own copies and do whatever we want with them. You don't even need to give credit to the original creators, although not doing so is what is known in the professional world as a "dick move." Anyway, I stole a bunch of the following words from Lewis Carroll's 1865 novel Alice in Wonderland, mixed them up a bit, and gave it my own spin. Did you know that the famous "we're all mad here" line doesn't come from the Mad Tea Party chapter?

There was a table set out under a tree in front of the house, and the March Hare and the Hatter were having tea at it: a Dormouse was sitting between them, fast asleep, and the other two were using it as a cushion, resting their elbows on it, and talking over its head. "Very uncomfortable for the Dormouse," thought Alice. "Only, as it's asleep, I suppose it doesn't mind."

The table was a large one, but the three were all crowded together at one corner of it: "No room! No room!" they cried out when they saw Alice coming.

"There's plenty of room! You just don't want me at the table," said Alice indignantly, and she sat down in a large arm-chair at one end of the table.

"Well spotted! Have some wine," the March Hare said in an encouraging tone.

Alice looked all round the table, but there was nothing on it but tea. "I don't see any wine," she remarked.

"There isn't any," said the March Hare.

"Then it wasn't very civil of you to offer it," said Alice angrily.

"It wasn't very civil of you to sit down without being invited," said the March Hare.

"I didn't know it was your table," said Alice; "it's laid for a great many more than three."

"There is empty space, but how does that concern you?" inquired the Hatter. He had been looking at Alice for some time with great curiosity, and this was his first speech.

"It's very rude to exclude someone," Alice said with some severity.

"Perhaps, but it's ruder still to start an opium war with China simply because you want cheaper tea," countered the March Hare.

"Two opium wars, actually," snored the still sleeping Dormouse.

"I had nothing to do with that," protested Alice. "I am merely a British subject, not a leader of state."

"And yet you arrived uninvited at our tea party," continued the Hare.

The Hatter opened his eyes very wide on hearing this; but all he said was, "Why is a raven like a writing-desk?" The March Hare glared at this blatant attempt at defusing the conversation but said nothing.

"Come, we shall have some fun now!" thought Alice. "I'm glad they've begun asking riddles.—I believe I can guess that," she added aloud.

"Do you mean insult by addressing us in the third person? We're immediately to your front and can hear what you're saying," the March Hare grumbled. "At any rate, by believing that you can guess, do you mean that you think you can find out the answer to it?" said the March Hare.

"Exactly so," said Alice.

"Then you should say what you mean," the March Hare went on.

"I do," Alice hastily replied; "at least—at least I mean what I say—that's the same thing, you know."

"Not the same thing a bit!" said the Hatter. "You might just as well say that 'I see what I eat' is the same thing as 'I eat what I see'!"

"You might just as well say," added the March Hare, "that 'I like what I get' is the same thing as 'I get what I like'!"

"You might just as well say," added the Dormouse, who seemed to be talking in his sleep, "that 'I breathe when I sleep' is the same thing as 'I sleep when I breathe'!"

"This all sounds like a tedious lesson in formal logic rather than a real conversation," said Alice, raising an eyebrow.

"How dare you! How dare you!" spat the Hatter. "Formal logic is fascinating and of great import!"

"Not the way you teach it, it's not," retorted Alice. "You've merely told me what you think I've done wrong, with no attempt to explain why believing I can guess is worse than thinking I can answer."

"You should be able to work that out yourself," said the

March Hare, snatching an empty teacup and slurping noisily.

"That's lazy and ineffectual pedagogy. All you're doing is claiming to be an expert and stating that I'm wrong without doing any work. You've placed the onus on me to learn without taking up the responsibility to teach," said Alice, swiping an equally empty teacup from the table and slurping even more loudly than the Hare.

"It's not true that they're doing no work," yawned the Dormouse. "They're working quite hard at protecting the patriarchy."

Here the conversation dropped, and the party sat silent for a minute, while Alice thought over all she could remember about ravens and writing-desks, which wasn't much.

The Hatter was the first to break the silence. "What day of the month is it?" he said, turning to Alice. He had taken his watch out of his pocket, and was looking at it uneasily, shaking it every now and then, and holding it to his ear.

Alice considered a little, and then said, "The fourth."

"Two days wrong!" sighed the Hatter. "I told you butter wouldn't suit the works!" he added looking angrily at the March Hare.

"It was the best butter," the March Hare meekly replied, staring at the hair-covered lump of cream upon the butter dish.

"I think the time has quite passed for declaring things to be the best when they're of obvious inferiority," the Hatter grumbled. "Although, it does sound somewhat presidential."

"It sounds more like the tune of a snake-oil salesperson to me," Alice remarked.

The March Hare took the watch and looked at it gloomily: then he dipped it into his cup of tea, and looked at it again: but he could think of nothing better to say than his first remark, "It was the best butter, you know."

Alice opened her mouth, seeking to trump the Hare's obvious lie when she was a little startled by seeing the Cheshire Cat sitting on a bough of a tree a few yards off.

The Cat only grinned when it saw Alice. It looked good-natured, she thought. Still, it had very long claws and a great many teeth, so she felt that it ought to be treated with respect.

"Cheshire Puss," she began, rather timidly, as she did not at all know whether it would like the name; however, it only grinned a little wider. "Come, it's pleased so far," thought Alice, and she went on. "Would you tell me, please, which way I ought to go from here?"

"That depends a good deal on where you want to get to," said the Cat.

"I don't much care where—" said Alice.

"Then it doesn't matter which way you go," said the Cat.

"—so long as I get somewhere," Alice added as an explanation.

"Oh, you're sure to do that," said the Cat, "if you only walk long enough."

Alice felt that this could not be denied, so she tried another question. "What sort of people live about here?"

"In that direction," the Cat said, waving its right paw towards the Hatter, "a mad person: and in that direction," waving the other paw, "a mad March Hare."

"But I don't want to go among mad people," Alice remarked.

"Oh, you can't help that," said the Cat. "We're all mad here. I'm mad. You're mad."

"How do you know I'm mad?" said Alice.

"How do you know you're not?" said the Cat.

Alice didn't think that proved it at all; however, she went on, "And how do you know that you're mad?"

"To begin with," said the Cat, "a dog's not mad. You grant that?"

"I suppose so," said Alice.

"Well, then," the Cat went on, "you see, a dog growls when it's angry, and wags its tail when it's pleased. Now I growl when I'm pleased and wag my tail when I'm angry. Therefore, I'm mad."

"I call it purring, not growling," said Alice.

"Call it what you like, " said the Cat, "but I'm doing the opposite of a thing that's not mad."

"But that doesn't make you mad!" argued Alice. "That assertion only works if growling and tail wagging is what makes a creature not mad!"

"I knew you'd figure out formal logic!" crowed the March Hare.

"You didn't plan for this outcome, you credit-thieving foozler!" insulted Alice.

"Fuck you, colonizer," jabbed the Hare, who then lashed out with his empty teacup, violently spilling nothing onto Alice.

Alice leapt atop the table and upended an entire teapot of nothing onto the Hare, accidentally spilling much of it onto the Dormouse, who would have been badly scalded had he been conscious. He instead snoozed lightly, entirely unaffected by the furious display.

Polyphemus' Bad Day

Centuries ago, legends walked the Earth. Among their names were Nezha, Rama, Kintaro, Thor, and Odysseus. This is not one of their stories.

Look, there are plenty of stories of them if you want to read them. I'm not stopping you from doing it. I'm just saying that I don't have any here.

Okay. Fine. Odysseus *does* have a cameo here, but that doesn't make it an Odysseus story!

Anyway. On with the tale.

"One! Two! Three!"

With combined, brutal force, Odysseus and his men dug their feet in, propelling themselves forward. On their shoulders sat a sharpened ship's plank that the cyclops Polyphemus used as a roasting spit. Though it weighed hundreds of pounds, desperation and Odysseus' honeyed words gave them the strength to charge at the sleeping cyclops. Together, they drove their makeshift spear into—look, this part is gross. I'm just going to gloss over it. No one needs to read me describing a violent blinding.

Bereft of sight, Polyphemus swung his arm around, dashing one of the men[1] against the cave wall. Swinging it back, he grasped another and crushed that man, too. The rest of the men fled the maimed giant in fear. Bellowing in agony, Polyphemus stumbled forward, leaning against the massive boulder that served as the cave's door. With a massive arm, he shoved it back far enough to yell for help.

"Help! Help! I've been attacked! I've been blinded!" he howled into the night.

After a few moments, other cyclops began to shout back panicked questions.

"Who attacked you?"

"How many?"

"Are you sure?"

To anyone who has screamed for help from their neighbors before, these questions should seem both familiar and infuriating. Not one of the titanic men asked, "How can I help?" Nor did any state plainly "I'll be right over to help!" People decry the lack of hospitality of the modern age, but it's always been like this.

"Noman has blinded me!" screamed Polyphemus.

"If no man blinded you, then you're probably fine," shouted a neighbor.

"If no man blinded you, maybe you're just sick," said another.

"If no man blinded you, perhaps you're not really blind," offered a third.

Some of you are starting to wonder aloud, "Hey, wait a

---

1 Hey. You ever noticed how none of Odysseus' men have names? Considering how many pages in the Iliad were devoted to cataloging everyone present, it's pretty weird that Homer didn't name anyone in Odysseus' party; it's almost like Odysseus himself didn't know, viewing all of his subjects as faceless, interchangeable cogs in a machine.

minute. Why *didn't* any of Polyphemus' neighbors come over to see what was going on or to help? After all, Polyphemus was a prince and a son of Poseidon. He was a pretty big deal and blowing him off is really weird." The answer is the same as any of the character actions throughout the epic: everyone in the Odyssey is an asshole. No. Really. Read it again. Find me someone who wasn't a dick.

"Have you tried losing weight or starting yoga?[2]" was the last thing Polyphemus heard before he gave up and rolled the boulder back in place, sealing the cave.

"BAAAAAA!" Polyphemus' herd of sheep had been crying out in a panic since he was blinded. His violent thrashing in the wake of the attack had done nothing to calm them down. He held his hands up and tried to shut out the sounds for a moment before deciding that there was no way he could concentrate while they bleated.

Reaching down for the nearest crying sheep, Polyphemus wrapped his hand around the top and lifted it up, pleased that this particular type of food wasn't trying to kill him. He shuffled back to the entryway, his feet moving in a way he thought was erratic enough to kick or crush anyone who tried to follow him. He pressed his hand against the boulder before thinking better of it and he swiped at the corners around the boulder, catching a man and flinging him back into the cave.

"You are clever, 'Noman,' but your crime will be punished," Polyphemus said as he pushed against the rock door again, moving it far enough to reach his other arm through. With his arm outside, he deposited a thoroughly confused sheep on the other side of the barrier and rolled the boulder back in place.

After repeating the process a few more times, every bleating sheep was on the outside of the cave, along with Odysseus, who had

2 OK, maybe I made that one up.

fearlessly leapt onto the first sheep and clung to its woolly belly without a word, bravely leaving all of his men behind to die. A few managed to escape the same way. The rest died over the course of the next few hours as Polyphemus crushed everything left breathing in the cave.

"Hey, Steropes, Arges, Brontes," Polyphemus said, greeting his brothers, who all stared at the bloodied wound that had been his eye. "Quick question: What the fuck is wrong with you? I got attacked last night, called out for help, and none of you assholes came to check on me."

"I'm really sorry. I, uh, thought you were just being dramatic. You were saying pretty weird things," offered Steropes, the Lightninger.

"Did you hear me scream?"

"Well, yeah."

"How far away do you live?"

"21 steps."

"You hear me scream and talk nonsense 21 steps away from you and you didn't even think to check on me?"

"When you put it like that, I—"

"Fuck you."

"I'm really sorry, brother. Look—uh … I mean, listen. I can go make a compress and mix some herbs for a poultice to put over your eye."

"I'm pretty sure it's gone," groaned Polyphemus.

"Maybe, but it might feel better," said Arges, the Thunderer.

"And, it would prevent infection and the pain that would bring," pointed out Brontes, the Vivid.

"Fiiiiine," signed Polyphemus.

Steropes and Arges thundered off to get the medicine ready

as Brontes helped his wounded brother to the ground, carefully placing rocks and massive bags of wool to ensure Polyphemus was comfortable. By the time Polyphemus had crushed or swept away everything that threatened to make his resting spot less than perfect, his brothers had returned with the rest of island's cyclops. They took turns checking in on their friend and seeing what they could do to make his life better in this troubling time. For the most part, the answer was food, wine, and more wine.

Being stabbed in the eye is ridiculously painful and it's not like there was a nearby pharmacy. Wine was the prescription and it got filled. And refilled.

"I brought you a cane!" said an older cyclops.

"I don't understand," puzzled Polyphemus.

"You can wave it in front of you like a longer arm. If you can't touch the ground, you're probably about to fall off of a cliff. If you hit something and it doesn't baa or say, 'Be careful, Polyphemus,' it's either a rock, a tree, or something you should hit harder."

"That's clever. I should have thought of that!"

"I wish I'd thought of it before I fell off the cliff the first two times!" the elder chuckled.

Polyphemus laughed until his eye hurt, which wasn't that long, honestly, but he did feel better.

Want Some T?

Eh? I'm just winding things up. Shutting it down. At least until the passes clear. Might be awhile. You, uh—if you don't mind me sayin' so—don't look like you're from here. Not that that matters a bit. Lots of folks from here leave and don't find their ways back here. Don't know how they're doin', but I'd imagine—I'd hope—that they found someplace else that suits them better. And other folks wind up here without knowin' exactly where here is and makin' it their home. What I'm tryin' to say here is that if you're meaning to stay here a spell, that's just fine. And if you're waitin' 'til the passes clear up so's you can make your way out somewhere else, that's okay in my book, too.

Not that you need my approval. You're a grown person. You can do as you please. That's somethin' most folks don't take to heart these days. Or any day, truth be told. Humans are social critters. We always want to make sure that what we do's okay in the eyes of other people. And, that's a good thing. It helps to make sure that we don't hurt no body.

We're still gonna do some harm. Ain't no gettin' 'round that.

Harm happens. Hurt happens. All we can do is try to keep it to a minimum. So, like I was sayin', you're your own person and you can do what feels right for you. If that means stayin' here when the weather gets better, well, plenty of space here for more folks.

And, hell, it don't even matter if you don't know whether you're stayin' or goin' right now, either. Or if you change your mind. Heh. I've been sayin' that this place isn't quite my home for years, but it's the closest thing I've found. It feels good. Solid. You say somethin' like that long enough and it stops being something you think about. It's just somethin' I say now. I know I'm not gonna up and leave here. I'm not too old to learn new things, but I know I don't want to find myself someplace that's not right again.

You know the feeling.

You sit down and everyone looks at you. Maybe they say that they're okay with you. Maybe they have daggers hidden behind them. Maybe the daggers are out in front, in plain view of anyone who thinks to look. Maybe everyone's fine, but only that: fine. Okay. Not bad. Not good. Things sit just well enough with you that you don't want to tear your heart out and cry your soul away. You can live like that. But you know in your heart of hearts that you don't want to. Something's gotta go. You or your surroundings.

I know you've felt that. I have. Hell. I—

No. We don't need to talk about that. If you want to later on, we can. But I don't need to know, and you don't need me to put any weight on your back by spillin' my guts before we even rightly know each other. Point is, there's a choice: move or don't. And "don't" means you don't make it, for the biggest definition of "make it." Self-harm, takin' one's own life, endin' it all, takin' the easy way out, suicide, whatever you want to call it.

Nothing easy about any of it. But, when you're a square block and all the holes around you are circles, the balls don't know you have it rough; they can go back and forth, no problems a'tall. Try as you might, you're not gettin' through those holes and it's no one's fault.

Whoever made those holes didn't know folks like you and me were around. Hmm? No. I don't blame them. They're just ignorant. They didn't know. They should'a. But, they didn't. If you tell 'em now? I don't know. Maybe they'll learn. Maybe they'll cut out a square hole and a triangle hole. Maybe they'll do the right thing and level out that playing field. Maybe they won't.

That's what being an activist is. Talkin' out loud and hopin'. Hopin' that someone'll listen and get those square and triangle holes cut. If you could do it yourself, that'd be even better, but not everyone can. It's hard. Too damn hard for me. You know what happens to most o' those folks who just do the work first without askin'? Well, they wind up in jail. Or worse. But, that's how fast change happens.

You know the first Pride was a riot? True story. Buncha trans ladies o' color got mad. Got real tired of bein' punished for not looking like balls. They were done being pushed around and started doing some pushin' of their own. Lotta people got hurt. Lotta people got arrested. Was it worth it? I think so. But I wasn't there. I wasn't one o' the ones getting hit by the cops. For me, it was just a story in the newspaper. It was just an action that started leading to folks like you and me not having to worry about as many of those daggers I was talkin' about.

Would I do it? Heh. I think we know now that I wouldn't. Or I'd be in jail right now. Does that make me a coward? I don't know. I hope not. I've spent my bravery doing other things. Some days, just gettin' up and lettin' other folks see my face is pretty brave. Maybe no one else thinks so. That's fine. They're not me. I know what it feels like to be me. It's hard bein' me all the time. But, that's why I'm here. Halfway between somewhere and somewhere else. Neither of those places'd suit me. But, here? In the neither here nor there? It's good. I like it.

Could it be better? Yeah. Probably. But I'd have to find that place first. And that's a whole mess of work that I know I'm not ready to handle. So, yeah. I'm home.

I hope this is your home, but if not, I hope you get there soon.

Want some tea?

The Gods of America are Dead

Content Warning: Suicide

No shit.

Not a single iota of shit.

If you had a shit detector with millishit tolerances, it wouldn't make a sound.

The fuck were we talking about?

Right. Yeah. Columbia's dead. Columbia? The Spirit of America? Yeah, she's dead. That's not a metaphor. Well — it is, and it isn't; it's both. Both the demigod Columbia and the ideals that she represents are dead. She came into being somewhere around 1796, along with the first paintings of her. She was radiant, gorgeous, and powerful. Fucking capital P Powerful. She had to be.

Back then, the newly-styled Americans dreaming her up had to compete with the disrespect that the British wanted to hurl at the idea of America. And if that sounds like the job of an old softy, you're very much mistaken. Don't get me wrong, the idea of believing a new god into existence in the same land where there are already hundreds of them is pretty silly.

The former colonists could have saved so much fucking time if they'd just turned to Great Spirit or K'uk'ulkan instead of reinventing the wheel. That's America for you, though. Land of "If it wasn't made here, fuck it." American-made is a whole identity for a lot of folks, which might be why Americans killed Columbia. The Spirit of America wasn't actually American-made; she was made from bits and pieces of half-remembered lore from the Greeks and Romans.

I mean, let's be real here. Americans of the time weren't even American; they were Aniyunwiya, Powhattan, Virginian, or Massachusettsers or whatever the fuck the demonym for people from Massachusetts is. America didn't exist anywhere except on paper, so it's not really that big of a surprise that Columbia didn't survive into the era of modern Americans.

Anyway, Columbia's dead, and so's Uncle Sam. Yeah, no, you'd think he'd be around here somewhere. His face sure is. We all know him and his catchphrase. "I want you!" Shit's iconic. But when was the last time you saw him out in the wild? When did you really get the idea that the country was going to roll up its sleeves and put in some work alongside you? When did you last feel like your uncle was gonna give you a hand in tough times, or box the ears off someone who was coming for you? The years after 9/11, right?

Yeah. That wasn't universal.

Everyone was spoiling to fight after 9/11 and sensed Uncle Sam standing up. The problem is that a lot of Americans thought Uncle Sam was coming after them. And he was. Hell, he'd been coming after Brown and Black folks for a long time. That Black Lives Matter stuff outside your window? Nothing they're saying is new. Those are the echoes of protests from generations ago. Things've gotten better since then, but Uncle Sam never treated Black and Brown folks right. After the Twin Towers fell? Anyone even a little bit tan or fluent in another language was a target.

How'd this inequity kill Sammy-boy? Well, gods need belief to survive, and Uncle Sam had plenty of it at that point. Pissed off people believed that he would crush the enemies of the US. Scared people believed he'd crush them. That's faith enough. Fear's faith. Just ask Kali. No, don't. Nevermind. Forget I said anything. At any rate, with that much belief fueling him, you know he didn't starve. So, what the hell happened to him?

After US forces ground to a halt in Iraq and Afghanistan, they just sort of sat there, holding onto checkpoints and playing whack-a-mole with the few militants who popped their heads up, both sides killing civilians because they didn't trust anyone who didn't look like them. Operation Iraqi Freedom became OIF 1, then OIF 2 and 3. The generals kept talking about phases, but all anyone saw was literal lines in the sand being blown away by the desert wind. It wasn't the great military victory the hawks were spoiling for.

So, the blood-thirsty Americans stopped believing in ol' Sparklepants, leaving him almost entirely fueled by fear. You know what that's like? Being alone except for people who're deathly afraid of you? Can you imagine living knowing that you're the bad guy, that you're the boogieman that frightens children so much they cry themselves to sleep, not daring to peek out of their covers for fear that you'll get them? That's not what Uncle Sam was stood for, so he tied a rope around his neck and stopped standing.

Uncle Sam hung himself in the Alamo. It took a week for him to die.

In the vacuum, people stopped believing in gods and ideas and started putting their religious fervor in people. Any historian worth their salt can give you a long list of reasons why that's a terrible idea. Some believed in a Black man, others in the destruction of the same man. The one who'd stood behind Uncle Sam hoping to sacrifice blood for power were in the latter camp; they traded their anger of stateless terrorists for hatred of their neighbors.

Do you understand the power of hate? The worship power created by wanting to unmake someone? It's like a cloud made by boiling venom. Like all clouds, what they worshipped could look like anything. Sooner or later, they had no idea what they were doing, only that they liked worshipping and wanted to keep at it. So, they bowed down to whatever was in front of them. And they hated.

They hated. Haaate.

Science? They hated it. Hope? Hate. Equality? H A T E D

Next thing you know, deadly bits of the air in 2020 killed as many as a hundred 9/11s. Thanks for that, you fuckers. Your worship of the poison cloud fucked up everything. We still have hundreds of other gods here in the US, but with Columbia and Uncle Sam dead, the American gods are fading out. Which brings me to the next bit of bad news. You know that goddess with the scales and blindfold? Big-ass sword? Hangs out in front of courthouses?

Justice is on life support.

That sounds really dramatic and metaphorical, but it's not. The goddess Lady Justice has chemical pneumonia. Turns out getting gassed by the police every day for months is bad for everyone. She's still conscious and lucid for now. She's not even mad at the cops. They're her kids just as much as everyone who walks out of a courthouse is. She can't be mad at them, but she is disappointed.

One of her children in blue kills. Another of her kids holds up signs and spits in a blue kid's face. Tear gas flies. Blast balls detonate. A child in blue kills again. It's a bad fucking time for Lady Justice and her children. If she could get her blue kids to stop killing, there might be a chance to right the ship, but that's not going to happen as long as people keep bowing down to the Venom Cloud.

We can and should still believe in Justice even if we don't believe in the system that builds statues to her. Maybe even especially if we don't believe in the system. Without Justice, there's no America. That idea's baked into every protest.

No Justice.

No Peace.

When we stop believing in her, we stop believing that people have rights. We stop believing that society exists. And, for many marginalized folks, civil society's barely a whisper of a promise. If they lose that, if we take that away from them, they have nothing but the strength of their own arms keeping them safe. For many, that's practically a death sentence. If we don't fight for Justice, not only is there no reason to not burn it all down, there's actually several compelling reasons to slap the button marked "Vive la Révolution!" And that brings us to America's last god standing, the French immigrant: Lady Liberty.

Unlike all of the other American gods, she's doing just as fine as ever, relatively speaking. She stands on her pedestal, broken chains at her feet, and stares out at the Upper Bay. She's a symbol of freedom, a welcoming sight to anyone traveling to Manhattan by sea. And she's miserable.

Decades ago, she stood powerless as planes slammed into the World Trade Center behind her. In the months afterwards, she saw the Venom Cloud's rise to power. She watched it happen and did what she could to preserve civil liberties, but standing firm wasn't enough. It never is. She promised freedom, but the Poison Cloud offered patriotism, the ability to lash out at an unjust world. As the memories of boats headed past her to Ellis Island fade, she cries, mourning the echoes of an America that was less obsessed with power and control. Her tears fill the New York Harbor fifty feet deep.

And here we are, a present where the American-made gods are dead or nearly so. Sounds bleak, right? You're probably thinking that the Poison Cloud's won. But, that's not accurate. This isn't a battle between the gods. This is a battle between us and the gods. And we're winning; there's only one left, and we know how to fight hate.

We fight it with love, but not in the way that people usually think. You can't hug a Nazi so hard that they become something good. That's not the power of love, nor is it a realistic or fair scenario; victims of violence shouldn't need to forgive their abusers in order to live in peace. But we *can* raise everyone else up. Nazis are only bold when they have someone to stand on. When we take care of each, we're all the same height. And we outnumber the bullies. We'll never eradicate hate, but we can cover it in bubble wrap and smother its power.

81

Go help a soup kitchen. Defy curfew laws and food handling restrictions and give out sandwiches at a homeless encampment. Tell your crotchety relatives that Black lines matter. That trans lives matter. Donate to your friends who are struggling. Your donation doesn't need to be money to make a difference; sometimes kind words are all you can give and all anyone needs. Help each other. Stand up for each other's rights.

Four gods down.

One to go.

An Interview with Hiromi Cota

When did you start writing and why?

I started writing very early in life, although I'm certain that if I looked back at any of my early stuff, I'd hate it. I won an award for poetry at some point in middle school. It got printed in the school paper, which was probably the first time my work got published. What I can remember of the poem is awful, and I hope it stays lost in the pre-widespread-internet era. I wrote tons of short stories, comics, and novellas as a teen. They got increasingly better, but I hope none of that stuff resurfaces, either.

I'm a big believer in the idea that you get better at writing by doing a lot of it, as opposed to agonizing over the minutiae. It's a messy process, but the end result is a stronger writer. I'm better *because* I wrote a lot of garbage. I can recognize the flaws in what I've created and can avoid those pitfalls in the future. Had I focused on getting everything right the first time, that single work would be strong, but *I* wouldn't.

Why I started writing is much simpler; I had ideas in my head that needed to come out. It physically bothers me to hold onto an idea for too long. (And this is true of most folks. Persistent thoughts are referred to as rumination, which is linked to a number of behavioral disorders. Many theraputic methods encourage getting unloading those thoughts.)

Some thoughts are fleeting and go away on their own, but others are more interesting and persistent. I have to externalize those ones, or it'll affect my mood. If I have a tune in my head, I'll sing or beatbox. If I have a story idea or a fun quip, I need to write it down. Some of these things are entertaining enough to me that I want to work them into a story for other people to read.

Which authors or books influenced you the most as a writer?

Oh, hell. That's a long list. At some point of my childhood, I was challenged to read as many books as possible and, for a long time, I'd just eat novels — at least one a week, sometimes more than one a day; it was ridiculous. All the big names in sci-fi and fantasy went into the woodchipper that was my brain back then: Isaac Asimov, Douglas Adams, Anne McCaffrey, Robert Heinlein, C. J. Cherryh, Terry Pratchett, Roger Zelazny, Stephen R. Donaldson, Ursula K. LeGuin, Frank Herbert, Orson Scott Card, the list just goes on forever.

And that doesn't even cover the wider world of books I got access to as an adult, like the works of Octavia Butler, N. K. Jemisin, and Jessica Hagedorn.

Trying to pick which influenced me the most is like picking which drop of water in the ocean is my favorite. So, instead of a direct answer, I'll cheat: Mary Shelley invented the genre of science fiction by writing *Frankenstein*, making her the most influential author to me.

Which authors or books had the biggest impact on you as a person?

Fuck.

I should have read all the questions before sitting down to answer them. Well, no one reads these because they want a formulaic answer; they read them to get a sense of who authors are, so you readers get to see me somehow paint myself out of this corner. You also get to learn that I have an above-average level of profanity. I was infantry for 8 years, and "swearing like a sailor" is not at all limited to the Navy.

At any rate, I'd say it's a toss-up between Douglas Adams,

Terry Pratchett, and Stephen R. Donaldson.

DNA ("Douglas Noel Adams" sometimes gets abbreviated to "DNA" among fans since "DNA" is shorter than "Douglas Noel Adams" or even the cover version of his name "Douglas Adams." So, I'm using "DNA" purely for brevity's sake) wrote a wide range of characters into his stories and made most of them likeable. Marvin, the paranoid android, has deep psychological disorders, which doesn't prevent him from being cool. As someone with chronic depression, that was reassuring to see.

Terry Pratchett wrote extensively about the inequities of society and life, crystalizing a lot of concepts for me. He made it clear that society is made stronger through diversity and through looking out for one another. A dog-eat-dog world is a dead end.

And Stephen R. Donaldson wrote a bunch of very well-written assholes. I did my best to not end up like them. I was definitely an asshole in my early 20s, but I'd like to think that I've become a much nicer person since then and that I've managed to avoid being as bad as Thomas Covenant or Angus. I mean, I've definitely been better than Angus; that's a ridiculously low bar.

Which of your original twelve Prompt stories are you most pleased with?

Oh, that's tough. I think January's "Inside the Blue Circle" is one of my strongest. A homeless, gender-fluid wizard couple that break time to see what'll happen? How can you not love that? On top of that, I got to play with typography to cleanly delineate between the genders as the characters shifted their moods.

The names @ and & were natural extensions of Alfred Bester's typographical experiments with showing telepathy in prose in his 1953 novel *The Demolished Man*. In that book, several characters have their names partially represented through symbols, like ¼maine instead of Quartermaine or Wyg& instead of Wygand. I took it two steps further by using symbols as the nuclei of the characters' names, which can then form the basis for gendered varients of their names. Thus, when @ feels femme, she's N@alie. When they feel masculine, he's M@. Special shout out to Professor Tom Foster who had me read *The Demolished Man* during my undergraduate work.

@ and & are such fun characters that I've been working on a

novella series for them to get into further mischief and break more rules. It's much further behind than I'd like, partially due to overloading myself with projects and partially due to the pandemic. They should come out the same year you read this, which isn't too bad of a wait.

Which of your original twelve Prompt stories did you find the most difficult to write?

May. Hands down.

My story for May wasn't originally "Be Fae! Do Crimes!" I was originally going to write something much darker and personal, about how the criminal justice system's thirst for closed cases and "good" statistics has a human cost that kills people and ruins lives. 2019 wasn't a big year for Black Lives Matter protests, but that didn't mean that police violence wasn't on my mind.

My original story took the subject of police violence seriously and was fucking heart breaking to write. I felt like I had to do right by the people directly harmed by police, and that's an impossible weight to carry. So, with a few days to go before my deadline, I took an entirely different approach to the same subject; I made it a power fantasy where this fae changeling got to do whatever they wanted, and the cops couldn't hurt them. The fae creature got to just live without having to worry about getting shot or clubbed or gassed, and who doesn't love the idea of being able to live without being hurt?

"Be Fae! Do Crimes!" was *way* easier to write than what I originally set out to do.

What book on writing do you recommend?

I've already hedged a lot and answered questions like this with, "There are a lot of books." So, of course I'm going to give a complex answer for this.

Read many books on writing. There's no one step, one-size-fits-all solution to being a better writer. If there were, there'd be no market for books on writing; we'd all buy the same book and be done with it.

We write different things and our brains work differently. I'm not even talking about neurotypical vs. neurodivergent writers, although that's certainly something to consider (and I suspect the professional writing community has a disproportionately large number of neurodivergent folks compared to the rest of the population; creatives are weird. We just are.)

If I process ideas differently than you do, it'll be a massive pain to get you to follow my writing process. I know this for a fact because I've been an adjunct English professor, a magazine editor, and a book developer. I've taught writing a bunch of different ways; it's not easy, and neither is learning how to write.

What works for one person may not work for someone else. So, avoid this problem entirely by not reading just one book on writing. Read a bunch of them. Take all the techniques and tips from them all and figure out what works for you. If you run across a tip that doesn't work for you, you don't have to put it in your toolkit.

And don't just read writing books for your genre. I get it. Books are expensive, and time is precious. But, read everything you can get your hands on. Make full use of your local library.

What advice would you give an unpublished writer?

Write garbage. **Write a lot of garbage.**

Acknowledge that your first few projects aren't going to be great. Give yourself the freedom to suck. And then write garbage. It won't be good stuff, but it'll be *your* words on a page. The more you write, the more you develop your voice and — hopefully — the more you recognize what you're good at and what you need to improve at.

Once you have a pile of words, you can fix what you don't like, you can find treasure to be used in a different project, or you can write something entirely new that's better than your first stab at it. You have options. But, write garbage first.

When you have something that you think is great, try pitching it to someone. You might get a rejection notice, but — look. There are a lot of authors out there who were still in their "write garbage" phase when they sold their first story by being in the right place at the right time. If you think you have a story worth reading, pitch it.

Do you have a "dream project" as a writer? What would it be?

It's probably no surprise that my initial instinct is to answer this with, "I have many dream projects." But, on reflection, I can actually narrow that down to a goal that's both abstract enough that I can share it and tangible enough that it can make sense to others.

I want to do what Terry Pratchett did; I want to develop a world rich with difference to allow a wide spectrum of tales to be told, critiquing society through the lens of humor. With a whole world in play, every aspect of our world is available for examination.

In the past, I've tended towards shorter work, which allows me to create worlds that readers only ever see a slice of. I work hard to make those worlds feel real and lived in, but I think it'd be satisfying for readers (and me) to stick around in a single world for a few years and get a real sense of it. These books would give folks frequent vacation in another world instead of a brief stopover like I've been doing.

The original twelve Prompt stories were written in 2019. In 2020 we all experienced a global pandemic. Did the pandemic impact your writing? How?

Uuuuuuuggggggggggghhhhhhhhhhhhh (groan noises)

Yes. Yes, it did. In January 2020, I working on five roleplaying games, two plays, and three fiction series. I've had the shelve the fiction because it's so much harder for me to create worlds whole cloth than it is for me to write tens of thousands of worlds for a world that already exists. I also had to shelve the plays because we can't perform them anywhere. Getting the RPGs written was rough, but I did it.

Honestly, RPGs are pretty much the only thing that I've been able to write this year. The pandemic consumes a huge amount of mental energy because so many things are either impossible or ill-advised. On top of that, the news is a constant source of alarm because our soon-to-be-ex-president is consistently terrible. When presented with two options — each with their own pros and cons — he finds a third option that's even worse than the options that were on the table. As of this writing, 22 November 2020, we're at 256,000 COVID-19-related deaths in the US. And, that only covers the deaths directly related to the virus. It doesn't cover ancillary deaths caused by increased psychological and physical stress or from scarcity of medical treatment.

On top of that, both my spouse and roommate work from home now, which means that we each have to carve out our own space and time to work, which means we all mildly interfere with each other. And, we're well aware that this makes us lucky. Millions of folks have jobs that force them to stay out in public spaces and risk exposure to the virus.

It's a terrible year for everyone, but especially service workers.

Tip them. And keep tipping them after the pandemic is over. They deserve every penny.